LOVE, TRIANGLE

Written by **Marcie Colleen**  Illustrated by **Bob Shea**

BALZER + BRAY
An Imprint of HarperCollinsPublishers

With love to the other three
sides of the Quadrangle:
Kat, Joyce, and Amber

—M. C.

For Colleen

—B. S.

Balzer + Bray is an imprint of HarperCollins Publishers.

Love, Triangle
Text copyright © 2017 by Marcie Colleen
Illustrations copyright © 2017 by Bob Shea
All rights reserved. Manufactured in China.

Library of Congress Control Number: 2016952702
ISBN 978-0-06-241084-9

Typography by Dana Fritts
17 18 19 20 21 SCP 10 9 8 7 6 5 4 3 2 1
❖
First Edition

Ever since they were a dot and a speck,

Circle and Square's friendship had a shape of its own.

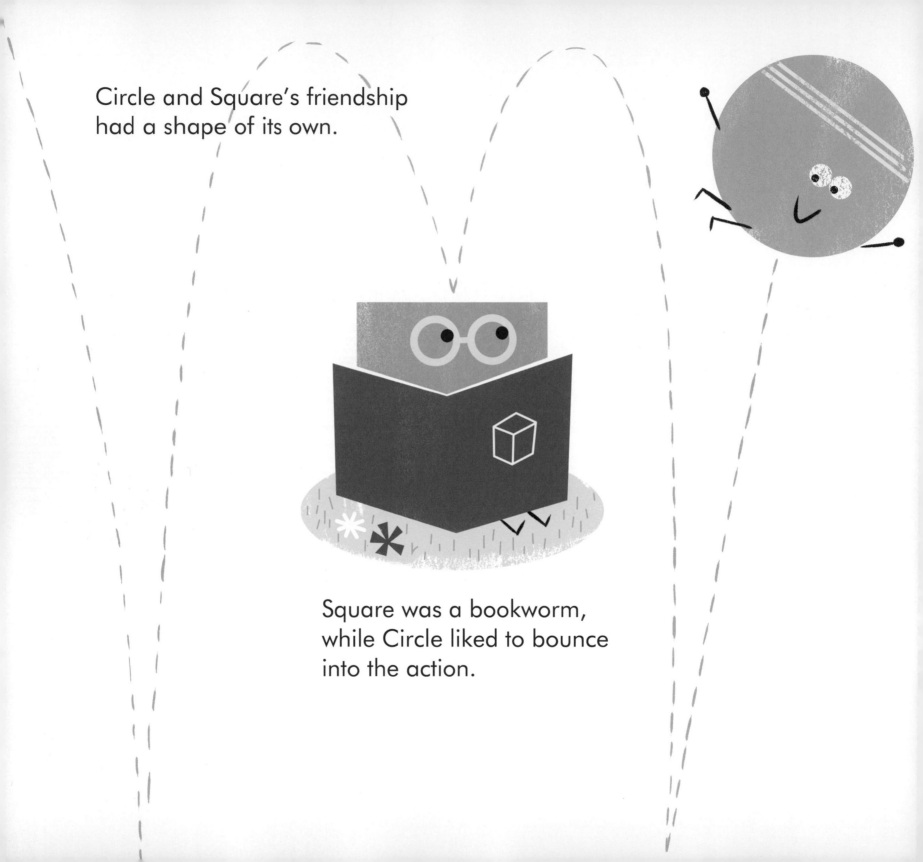

Square was a bookworm, while Circle liked to bounce into the action.

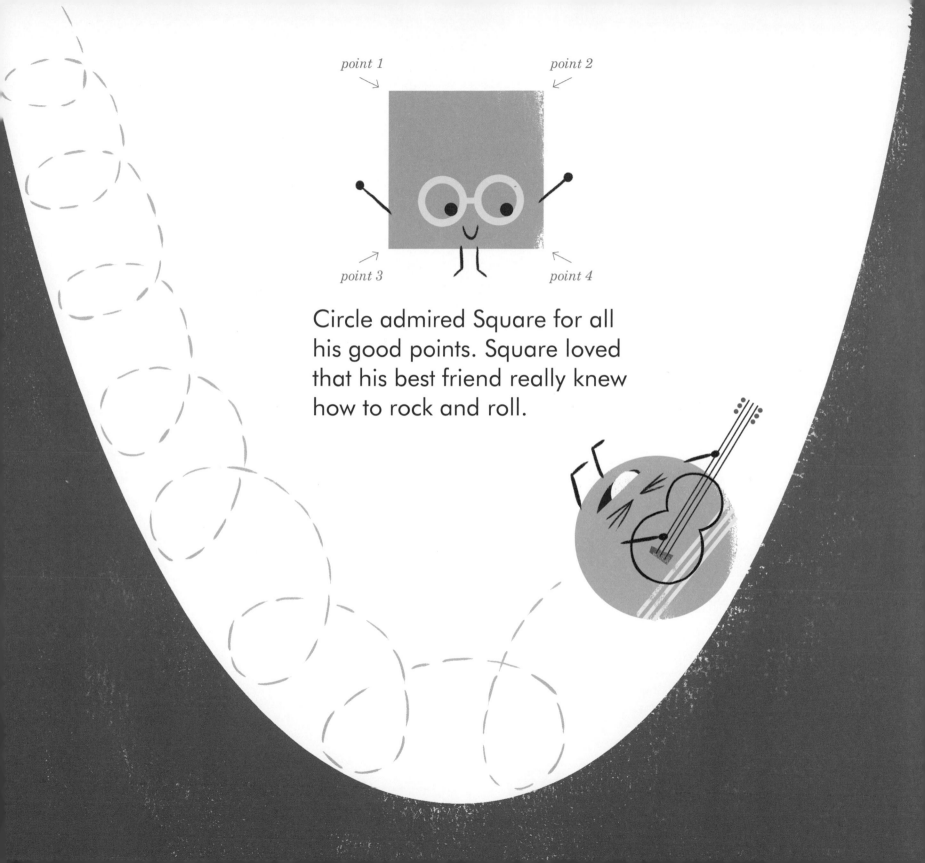

point 1 *point 2*

point 3 *point 4*

Circle admired Square for all his good points. Square loved that his best friend really knew how to rock and roll.

Until a wedge came between them.

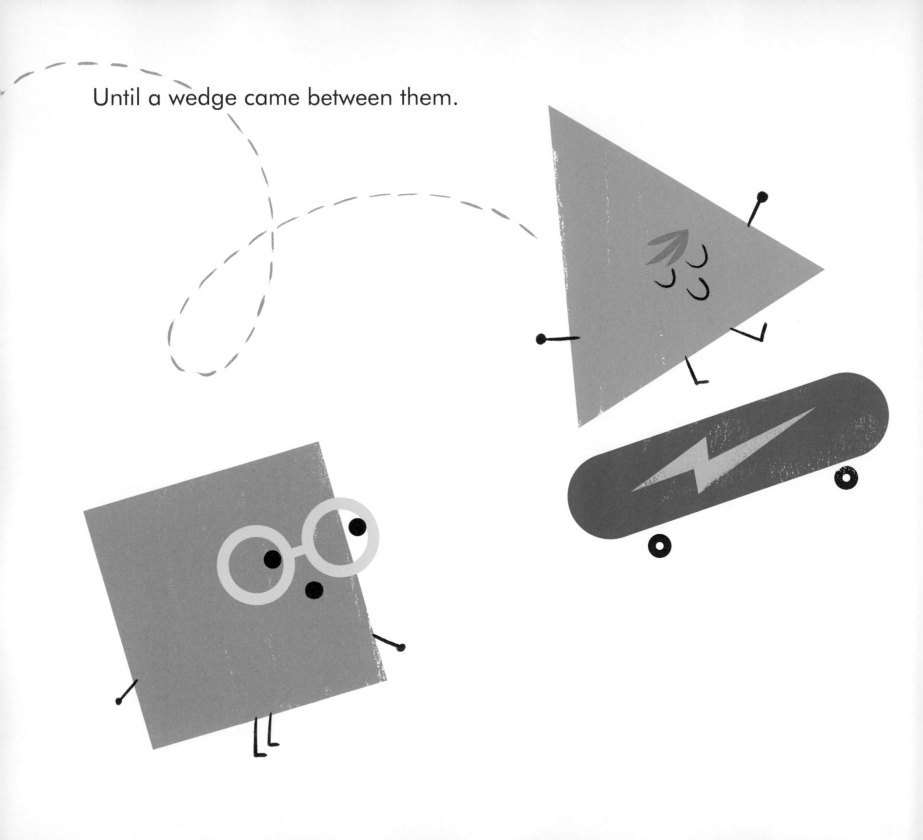

Well, not really a wedge.
More like a bold and
exciting Triangle.

At first small things changed, like lunch.

And at the library.

A new book about basketball!

Where are books on the
Egyptian pyramids?

Then bigger things.

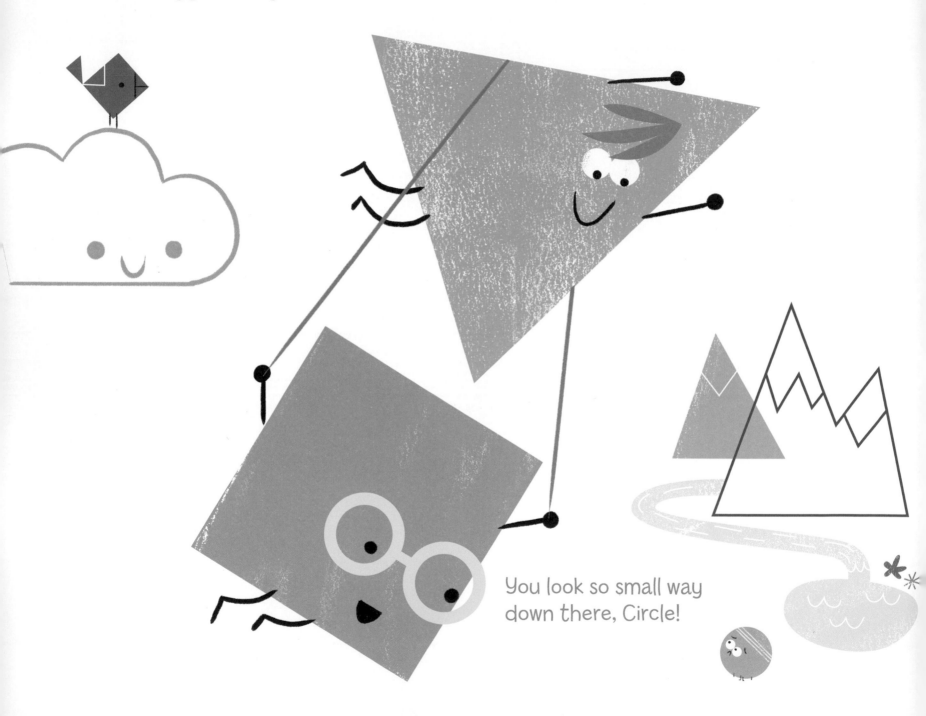

You look so small way
down there, Circle!

I am going to ace this test! Triangle,
you are the perfect study buddy.

I thought we . . . never mind.

Everything seemed to become triangular.

Triangle is so fast. He can dart quicker than anyone I know!

Triangle is so sharp. He's going to help me with my next project.

Triangle said he once soared higher than the birds.

Triangle said these are the kinds of shorts they wear in Bermuda.

Hey, guys! Do you want to play double Dutch?

I WILL!

NO! I WILL!

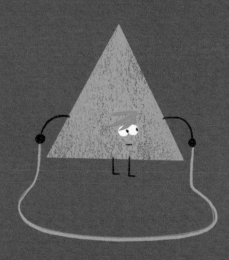

Why don't you ask your
BEST FRIEND!

Why don't you ask
your BEST FRIEND!

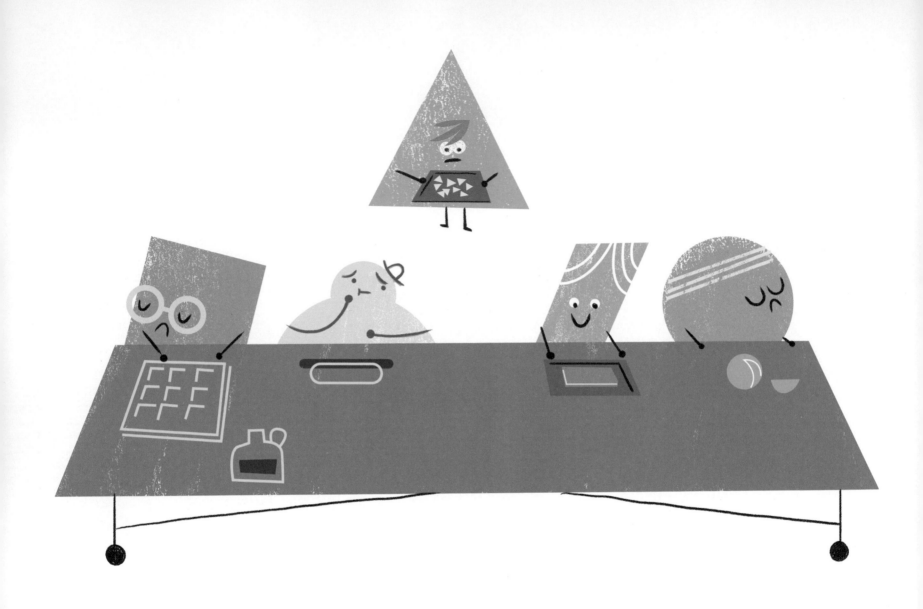

Circle and Square's friendship was bent out of shape.

Triangle decided something needed to be done.

Meanwhile, Square received something special of his own.

Come Saturday, they both showed up on Triangle's doorstep.

Wait. What are
YOU doing here?

WELCOME

Wait. What are
YOU doing here?

Needless to say, it was awkward.

Circle and Square stayed glued to Triangle's sides.

Grilled cheese, anyone?

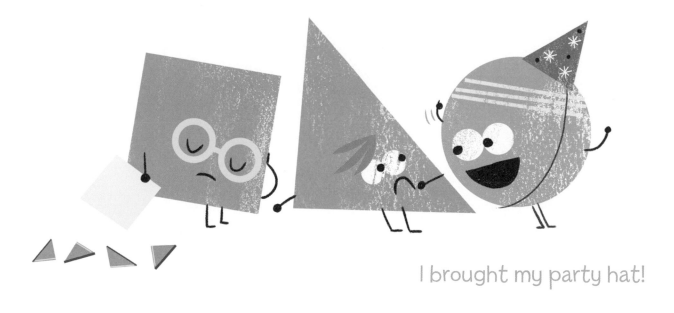

I brought my party hat!

Square blocked Circle.

Circle blocked Square.

Square pulled Triangle
one way,

Circle pulled Triangle
the other way.

Until . . .

Everything became pointless.

Look what you did!

Look what you did!

Triangle couldn't take it any longer.

_____

I've had it up to my APEX!
You both crossed the line!

Circle and Square panicked.

Circle grabbed one end of Triangle and raced around and around but succeeded only in making a mess.

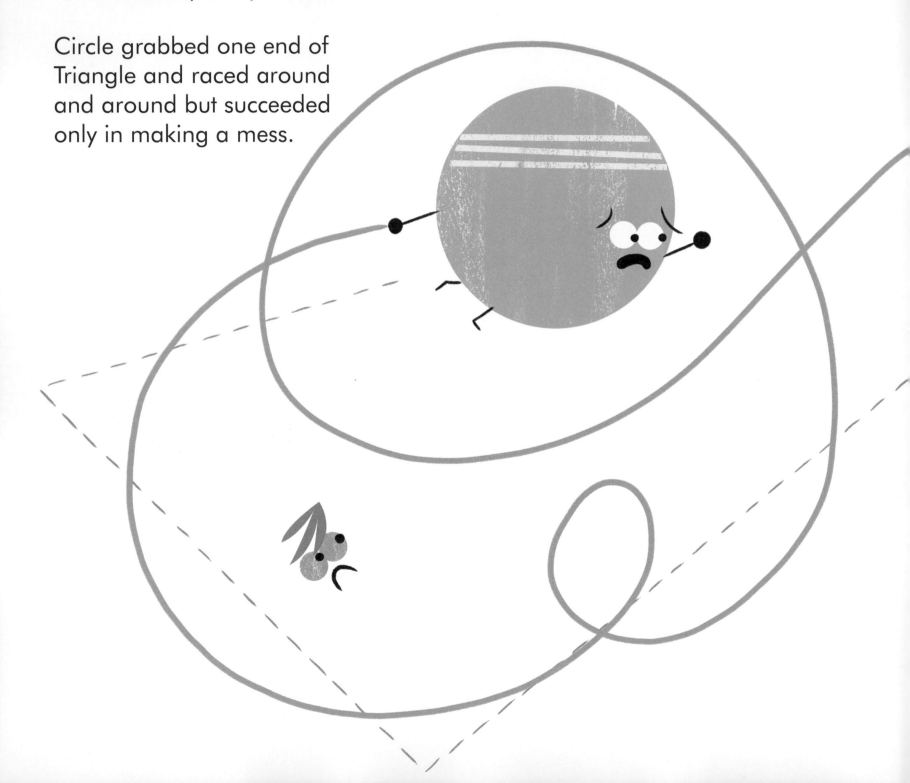

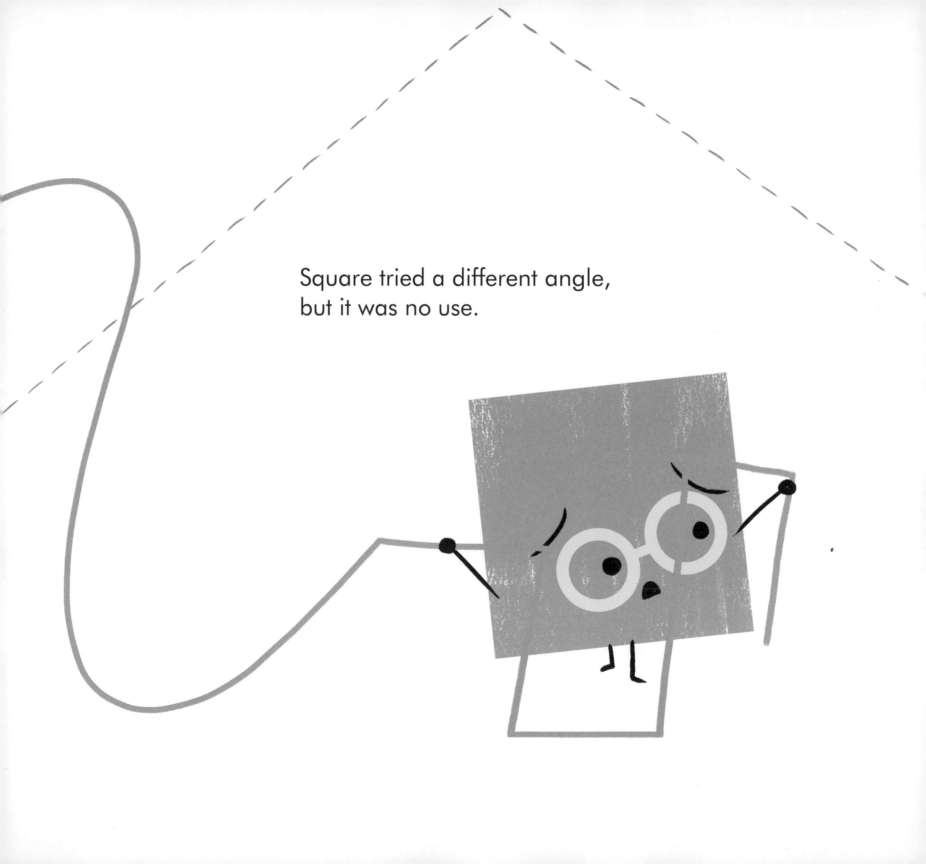

Square tried a different angle,
but it was no use.

They couldn't just leave Triangle like that.

Square buried his nose in research.

Circle practiced his moves.

And then . . .

I have an idea!

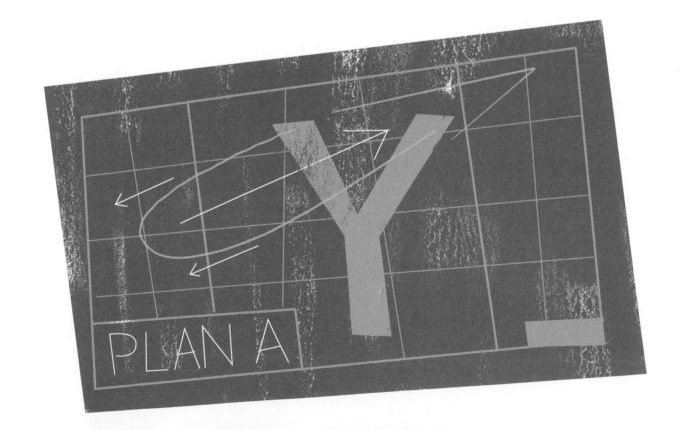

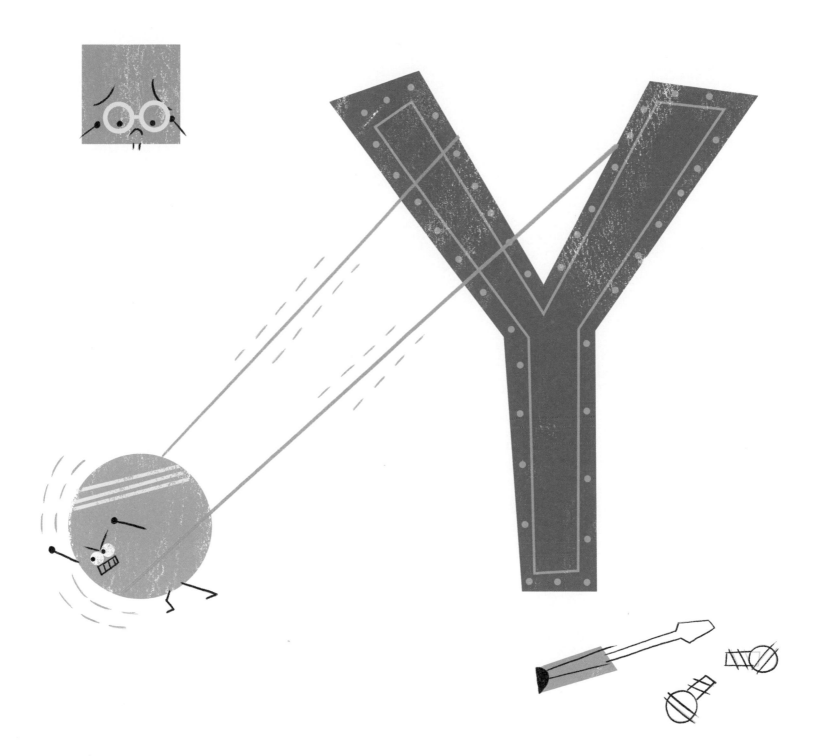

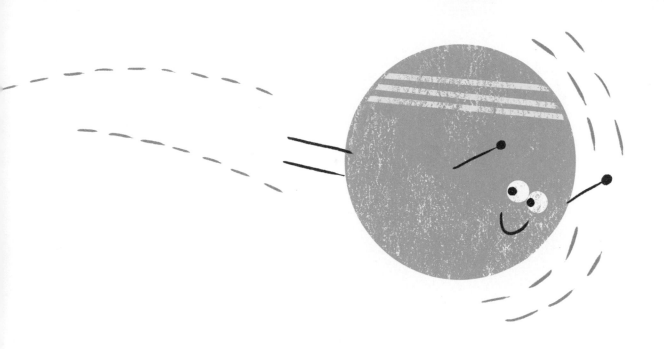

From that day forward, Circle,
Square, and Triangle's friendship
took on a shape of its own.